A
TALE
OF
TWO
RICE BIRDS

A
TALE
OF
TWO
RICE BIRDS
A Folktale from Thailand

Adapted by Clare Hodgson Meeker

Illustrated by Christine Lamb

SASQUATCH BOOKS
SEATTLE

In the center of Thailand,
where the Chao Phraya River flows,
there once lived two rice birds.
They built their nest in a teakwood tree
on a ridge between two rice fields.

The rice birds were small with plain brown feathers
that did not attract attention.
But when they flew close together,
their dark shadow made the farmers take notice.

When the rains came, the great river's floodwaters
turned the rice seedlings green and filled the lotus pond nearby.
Every morning, the two rice birds swooped and dove
for worms and tiny fish in the rice paddy pools.
And when they grew thirsty, they stopped to sip nectar from the lotus blossoms.
"We must stay only a minute," the female rice bird would warn her mate.
"The sun is high, and we don't want to be caught when the petals close."

The two rice birds drank nectar from the large cups of the lotus flowers
and then continued their search for food.
In time, the rice birds hatched three baby birds.
From then on, the father rice bird flew alone in search of food
while the mother rice bird stayed in the nest.

One morning,
when the sun was still low and red in the sky,
the father rice bird stopped at the lotus pond for a drink.
I will take one sip, he thought,
and then fly home to my family.

But one taste of the sweet nectar
made the father rice bird thirst for more.
He hovered and hopped from flower to flower,
forgetful of the rising sun.
When the sun shone directly overhead,
the lotus petals closed, trapping the rice bird inside.
He struggled to get out, but the petals were sealed shut.

Afternoon came.
The farmers left the white hot sun
to rest in the shade of the teakwood tree and eat their lunch.
Still the father rice bird did not return.
The mother rice bird fluttered anxiously around the nest,
wondering what could be keeping him.

Suddenly a spark from the farmers' coals set the tree on fire.

The mother rice bird beat the flames with her wings, but this only made the fire grow.

Soon the fire swallowed the nest.

The baby birds, still too young to fly, were trapped and turned to ashes.

When the moon rose and the petals opened in the cool night air, the father rice bird escaped.

He flew to the teakwood tree as fast as his wings would take him.

There, shivering on a blackened branch, was his mate.

"How could you have forgotten us?" she cried. "Our children died in this terrible fire. Now I wish to die too."

"But I did not forget you," said the father rice bird. "I was trapped in a lotus flower and could not escape."

"Lies, lies," said the mother rice bird. "If I am reborn a human, I will speak to no man again."

She lifted her wings and flew straight into the smoldering ashes.

The father rice bird raised his head to the dark sky and called to the gods, "I have always been a faithful husband.

Please let me follow her into the next life so we may learn to love each other again."

And he flew after his mate to his death.

The mother rice bird was reborn a princess
in a kingdom high in the mountains.
The king and queen were proud of their daughter.
She was a happy child, light on her feet
and eager to sing at any occasion.

When the princess grew to be a young woman,
she danced the *ramwong* gracefully, moving in a circle
close to the young men, though she never let her hands touch theirs.
The princess would laugh and play with other young women,
but she never spoke to men, not even to her father.
The king became worried.

He asked his daughter, "Why do you not speak to any man?
I am afraid that you will never marry and I will have no grandchildren."
The princess remained silent.

The king turned to the queen for help. "Issue a proclamation," she suggested.
"See if you can find a suitable man to match our willful daughter."

So the king issued a royal proclamation to kingdoms far and wide:
"Any man who can move the princess to speak shall be the one to marry her."

Meanwhile, the father rice bird had been reborn a farmer's son
in a village at the foot of the mountains.
When he was born, the rice fields bloomed
with green, fragrant flowers.
His parents believed this was a sign of good luck
and made an offering of fruit and sugarcane
to please the rice goddess.

Each year, the farmer's son helped his father
bring the rice to harvest.
When he was not needed in the fields,
he studied with a wise teacher, who also taught him magic.

One day, the teacher handed him the king's proclamation.
"You have learned everything I know," the teacher said.
"Now it is up to you to make your own life and follow your heart."

The farmer's son read the proclamation
and something deep inside him stirred.
"I will set off for this kingdom at once," he said.

When the farmer's son finally arrived at the king's palace,

he joined a procession of suitors waiting their turn to try to make the princess speak.

The first suitor came by elephant, carrying a bamboo cage full of *chingchokes*.

He opened the cage and the tiny lizards scurried out.

Then, drawing his bow, the suitor quickly trapped them behind a fence of arrows.

The king and his courtiers cried, "*Chai yo*," praising him for his marksmanship.

The princess said nothing.

Another suitor arrived by water buffalo, with a chest filled with precious jewels.

He threw the chest into the dark waters of the palace lotus pond and dove in after it.

When he reappeared with the chest and a lotus blossom crown on his head, the king laughed.

The princess frowned.

A third suitor brought a troupe of actors wearing bright silk costumes and hats with golden spires.

They performed a sad love story, which made the king and his courtiers cry.

But the princess did not shed a tear.

From the back of the great audience hall,
the farmer's son watched the proud, silent princess
and felt the flutter of love.
I must find a way to make her speak, he thought.

When his turn came, the farmer's son stepped forward
and bowed before the king, his hands clasped in front of his forehead.
The princess stared at the farmer's son.
He was so plain compared with the other suitors.
Just then, their eyes met and she felt her heart soar.
The princess rose and quickly left the room.

The king's eyes lit up.
"Can *you* move my daughter to speak?" he asked the farmer's son.

"*Chai,*" the farmer's son replied. "Yes, Your Highness.
I have learned to make my voice fly anywhere.
I will send it to speak with the princess, and hope she replies."

"Let us not waste a moment, then," said the king.
He led the farmer's son to the door of the princess' chamber.
"May good spirits accompany you," said the king,
and left him to his task.

The farmer's son used magic to throw his voice into the door.
Then the door spoke!
"I am the door to the princess' chambers.
The princess speaks to no man."
The princess had never heard her door talk before.
She tiptoed to the keyhole to listen.

The farmer's son said to the door,

"The night is long.

Perhaps you could help me pass the time with a story."

"I can do nothing but open and shut," replied the door.

"Why don't you tell *me* a story?"

"So I shall," said the farmer's son. He began:

"Once there were four friends—an astrologer, a hunter, a diver, and a magician.
One day the astrologer said to his friends,
'I predict that a large eagle will fly this way
carrying a young woman in its beak.'
The friends looked up and saw an eagle soaring high above them.

"The hunter drew his bow and shot the eagle.
A young woman fell from its beak into a raging river.
The diver jumped into the river and pulled her to shore.
But the young woman had swallowed too much water, and had died.
The magician then used his powers to bring her back to life."

"So," the farmer's son asked the door,
"which man do you think the young woman will marry?"
The answer is simple, thought the princess.
Even a door should know the answer.
The door replied, "She will choose the hunter.
Without him, the eagle would have carried her off."
The princess shook her head. Only a door could be so stupid.

"What about the diver?" asked the farmer's son.

"He rescued the young woman from the raging river."

"But without the magician," said the door, "she would be dead.

Surely the magician has an open-and-shut case."

Feeling as though her heart would burst,
the princess threw open the door and spoke.
"*Mai chai*, you are wrong," she exclaimed.
"The young woman will marry the astrologer,
because he knew of her coming
and planned her rescue."

"*Chai yo*," cried the farmer's son in delight.
"I hoped this story would make you speak.
Like the hunter, I saved you from unworthy suitors.
Like the diver, I traveled many miles to find you.
Like the magician, I brought your voice to life.
But most like the astrologer,
I planned for this moment.
I knew we were meant to be together
from a time long ago."

The princess smiled at the farmer's son, her dark eyes shining.
"I will honor my father's promise and marry you.
But love, like rice, takes time to grow.
Let us talk and come to know each other first."

The princess and the farmer's son spent many afternoons strolling in the palace gardens.
Together they watched the rice birds sip nectar from the flowers in the lotus pond.
And when their love blossomed, the farmer's son plucked a lotus and gave it to the princess.
"May this flower, which blooms again and again, be a symbol of our love."

The king gave his kingdom to the couple on their wedding day.
And from that time forward,
the princess and the farmer's son ruled
wisely and faithfully together.

All children in Thailand know the story of the two rice birds.
Whether told to them by a grandparent or read to them in school, this story helps
children learn about traditions and Buddhist beliefs that are important to the Thai culture.

Nearly three-fourths of the people of Thailand still live in rural areas and work the fields
in the traditional way of their ancestors. Rice fields and lotus ponds are familiar sights, from the
central plains to the hills in the north. Rice has been Thailand's major agricultural crop for centuries.
The rice-planting season begins in July, when heavy rains flood the fields. Throughout the hot, wet
fall season, farmers steer plows drawn by water buffalo and painstakingly transplant the tender
seedlings that will bloom and grow into tall stalks of rice. By November, when the winter season
begins, the rice is ready for harvest. The remains of the rice stalks are burned, and their ashes
are used to fertilize the fields.

Buddhism is the national religion of Thailand. Villages are built around red-and-gold-
painted temples, which serve as the center of spiritual and community life. Buddhism teaches that
if an individual is determined to reach a certain goal, he or she will eventually achieve it through
good deeds and good intentions. *A Tale of Two Rice Birds* weaves this idea together with the Buddhist
principles of reincarnation and enduring love. In the story, the father rice bird, mistakenly absent
when tragedy strikes his family, becomes determined to find his mate and prove his love for her.
He is reborn a farmer's son, and she, a princess. He sets out on a quest to regain her love. When
they eventually reunite, he presents her with a lotus blossom. In Thailand, the lotus symbolizes
Buddhism and is featured prominently in Thai art and architecture.

The illustrations for *A Tale of Two Rice Birds* are based on Thai mural art, a classic art form
commissioned by kings for the walls of temples and royal palaces. The mural art tells epic stories
of love and of famous battles against invaders from neighboring countries. The Thai people are
proud of the fact that their country has never been colonized by another people. In fact, the word
Thai, literally translated, means *free*. They believe that this stability and strength results from the
long line of kings who have ruled their country. Thai people often refer to the king as "my king,"
demonstrating their affection and reverence for the monarchy. The Thai king still resides in the
splendid, jewel-like royal palaces that were handcrafted centuries ago by thousands of Thai
artisans and laborers.

For my family.
— C.M.H.

To the memory of my grandmothers,
Georgia Bell Wilson Lamb and
Christine Anne MacKinnon Loranger,
who lovingly encouraged
my artistic pursuits.
— C.L.

The author and illustrator gratefully acknowledge
Supaporn Vathanaprida for her invaluable research assistance and support.

Published by Sasquatch Books
Distributed in Canada by Raincoast Books Ltd.

Printed in Hong Kong

Designed by Midge Williams

Library of Congress Cataloging in Publication Data
Meeker, Clare Hodgson.
A tale of two rice birds/by Clare Hodgson Meeker: illustrated
by Christine Lamb.
p   cm.
Summary: A Thai folktale in which a male and a female rice bird
die, but meet again when they are reincarnated as a farmer and a
princess.
ISBN 1-57061-008-8 : $14.95
[1. Folklore—Thailand.]   I. Lamb, Christine, ill.   II. Title.
PZ8.1.M474Tal   1994   94-552
398.24'528—dc20   CIP
                                                  AC

Sasquatch Books
1008 Western Avenue
Seattle, Washington 98104
(206) 467-4300